deep
down
blue

For my mom, who once taped a pretzel back together for me.
For Miriam and Coralie, who graciously provided plenty of reference for this book.
And for Nick, who helps me shake off my own angry layers.
—S. L. R.

STERLING CHILDREN'S BOOKS
New York

An Imprint of Sterling Publishing Co., Inc.
1166 Avenue of the Americas
New York, NY 10036

ISBN 978-1-4549-2858-4

Distributed in Canada by Sterling Publishing Co., Inc.
c/o Canadian Manda Group, 664 Annette Street
Toronto, Ontario M6S 2C8, Canada
Distributed in the United Kingdom by GMC Distribution Services
Castle Place, 166 High Street, Lewes, East Sussex BN7 1XU, England
Distributed in Australia by NewSouth Books
45 Beach Street, Coogee, NSW 2034, Australia

For information about custom editions, special sales, and premium and corporate purchases, please contact Sterling Special Sales at 800-805-5489 or specialsales@sterlingpublishing.com.

Manufactured in Canada

Lot #:
2 4 6 8 10 9 7 5 3
10/18

sterlingpublishing.com

Cover and interior design by Irene Vandervoort

The art for this book was created in Photoshop, using a Wacom Cintiq stylus/tablet.

Allie All Along

Sarah Lynne Reul

STERLING CHILDREN'S BOOKS
New York

SNAP!

Allie's crayon broke.

I blinked.

She was suddenly . . .

furious,
fuming,
frustrated,
and so, SO, SOOO

ANGRY!

She
stomped,
smashed,
crashed,
and threw

a tantrum,
a fuss,
and a fit.

I gave her a pillow to punch (so she wouldn't break other stuff).

That got the worst of the angry off.

Still,
Allie was
ferocious,
fierce,
and
VERY
ANGRY.

I asked her why, but she wouldn't say.

So I told her to squeeze her favorite toy as tight as she could. (He didn't mind.)

It looked like it
helped a little.

But Allie was still irritable and ANGRY.

Maybe she didn't even know why.

I feel that way, too, sometimes.

So I suggested,

"Try to take
a deep breath–

but don't hold
it too long!

Pretend that
my fingers are
candles . . .

. . . and you can

blow

them

out."

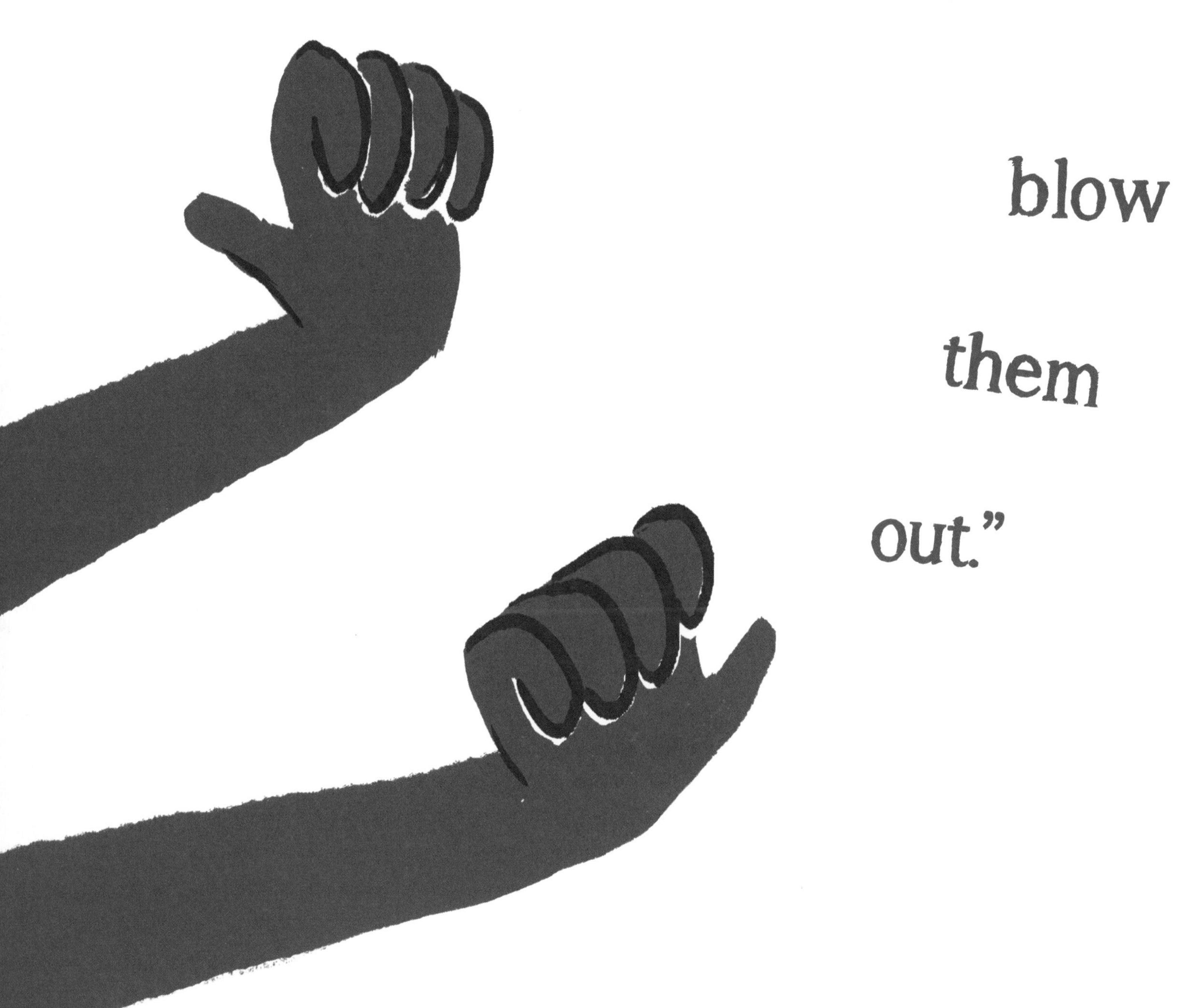

That seemed to help some more.

Then she
was just
plain old
regular
angry.

And maybe a little sad, too.

I helped her count backward from

The rest of the angry fell away . . .

. . . and there she was.

"Hug, please?"

I knew
she was in there
all along.